For the curious child in all of us
G.C.

For Mum, Dad and Paul
S.T.

Published in 2003 by Simply Read Books Inc.

Cataloguing in Publication Data

Crew. Gary. 1947-
The Viewer/Gary Crew:Shaun Tan. illustrator.

ISBN 1-894965-02-7

I. Tan. Shaun. 1974- II. Title.
PZ7.C876Vi2003   j823   C2003-910260-2

First published by Thomas C. Lothian Pty. Ltd.

Text designed and typeset by Lynn Twelftree
Printed in China by Toppan Printing Co.

THE
VIEWER

Ga   Tan

Simply Read Books

Tristan was curious from birth. This is not to say that he was different from other babies. In fact he was rather ordinary. But from the moment he opened his eyes, he seemed to be looking. Taking the world in, as it were. Nor did this remarkable curiosity — this constant need to search, to look out — lessen as he grew older.

From the time he was three years old, Tristan would wander from his parents' house, to be found — hours later, miles away, and always alone — staring up at a cloudless sky, or crouched by the seashore, peering at some long-dead life form that had been washed up there. Or once, in a city park, gathering the autumn leaves that lay scattered about him.

Another time — on an occasion when he vanished overnight — he was found in a museum, gazing into a display case of long-outdated cameras, oblivious of all else — even of the heartache that he had caused his parents.

But as he grew older and entered his teenage years, it was the city dump that attracted Tristan most. That was where he felt closest to his private view of heaven.

The dump stretched over acres of drifting sand, that arced like a yellow moon about the warehouses and factories and smoke-belching chimneys of the city. The place was littered with the off-scourings of a careless people. But to Tristan, each barbed and jagged coil of rusted wire was a chain of gold, each shard of splintered glass a diamond, each oozing slick of oil a rainbowed vein of fresh-cut opal.

From this treasure trove, he gathered the sad and broken objects he would take back to his room and store in the shadowy recesses of his dresser, or on the top of his wardrobe, or beneath his bed, until such time as his curiosity led him to look at them again, to pick them up and examine them. Finally, he would take them apart, determined to discover what had made them tick or whirr or ring.

And when he had restored them — his fingers deft and skilful, his eyesight sharp and focussed — he would place them on his desk and sit back, filled with wonder at the smooth and secret workings of the life inside. The world of levers and springs and cogs and gears — ticking, beating, throbbing, pulsing — an inner world that he could not see.

One Sunday afternoon, as Tristan was scavenging in the dump, he caught sight of a curious box among the rubbish, a box fashioned from dark wood and burnished metal. Its lid was covered in marks and scratches, which might have been names, or nothing more than ancient graffiti.

The lid of the box was hinged and latched, but the latch was held fast by a lock which he could not prise open, at least, not there at the dump, with the daylight fading. So he carried the box home, intent on discovering what secrets — what strange and wondrous objects — might be locked inside.

That night, after dinner, he removed the box from beneath his bed and placed it on his desk. He took a length of wire and a screwdriver, a fine silver jeweller's instrument, and triggered the lock. It sprang open with a sudden snap and he lifted the lid. He was struck by the musty odour of entombed air which crept from the dark space within to fill his room. To seep into his lungs.

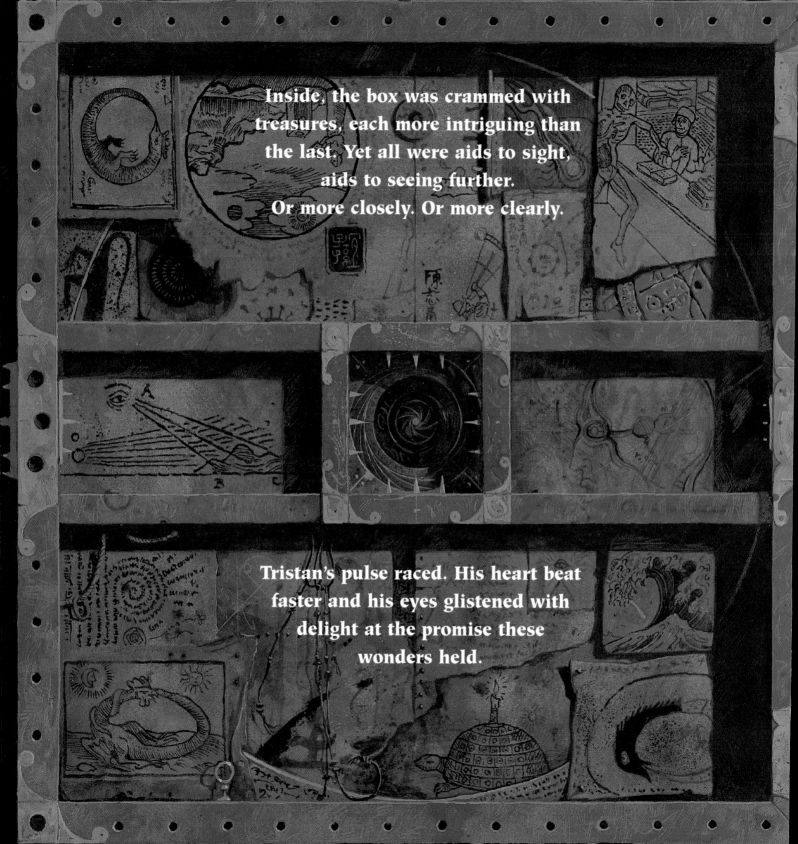

Inside, the box was crammed with treasures, each more intriguing than the last. Yet all were aids to sight, aids to seeing further.
Or more closely. Or more clearly.

Tristan's pulse raced. His heart beat faster and his eyes glistened with delight at the promise these wonders held.

What attracted him most was an object with two eye-pieces — like binoculars, he thought, although they were not binoculars exactly, not in the modern sense of the word.

He picked the thing up and held it to his eyes. It fitted him perfectly, as though it had been designed for his face, for the precise distance between his eyes. But he could see nothing. Only dark. Only two dark orbs.

He looked into the box again and there, in the shadow of a corner, were what appeared on first glance to be compact discs.

He took them out and looked at them. There were three, each enclosed in its own protective sleeve of yellowed paper. He removed one. It was as light as a feather, yet rigid. Its dull, metallic surface was cold. Icy cold. Cold enough to make him shiver.

Tristan smiled. Now he knew what this thing was. He had owned a toy something like it when he was a child: a Viewmaster.

He slipped the first disc into the machine and held it to his eyes. He pressed a lever at the side. There was a click which echoed ominously, like the sound of a lightning strike, and in an instant the darkness was gone.

But what he saw was like no picture he had ever seen.

Inside the machine, before his eyes, was a scene of fearful chaos.
The chaos of the beginning of a world . . .

He clicked again and the sound of the storm was silenced. He clicked again. And again. He heard the sound of the sea, the thrash and surge of waves and the moaning of a mighty wind. But above all, drowning all, came the chilling cry of an animal — something monstrous and beyond his knowledge, his imagining — but an animal all the same.

And then, though he hardly dared look, there followed the raucous cries of human beings, or what he thought were human beings, their voices raised in anger . . . and so he went on until the disc was finished.

Only then did he sit back, amazed, and breathing deeply.

He removed the first disc and reached for the next, inserting it with a trembling hand. He clicked again, and the mechanism whirred and snapped.

The second disc came to life. It was more peculiar than the first. Now, Tristan heard the grinding of stone against stone, the strain and stretch of mighty timbers. But still he looked, fascinated.

There followed the moaning of a wind, the slither and slide of sand, the drumming of torrential rain . . . and, after the rain, a stillness. And above the stillness, the wailing of people in distress, in fear of their lives.

When this disc was finished, he removed it and reached for the third.

This time he clicked more slowly, watched more carefully, and the sounds that he heard caused a shiver to creep up his spine. These sounds were softer — true — yet just as haunting. He heard the slow, even rhythms of a deep and distant drum, the lilt of chanting and the peel of a solitary bell. He heard the clash of steel upon steel, the thudding gallop of a thousand horses, and the human cries of those who fell beneath their hoofs.

These sights and sounds had made him terribly afraid. Still trembling, he took the disc out and the set the viewer down on his desk.

Then he crept into his bed, although he sensed, as he tried to sleep, that he was no longer alone.

The next morning he slept late, waking strangely tired. It was Monday, and that meant school. He glanced across at the box and saw the discs there on his desk, as he had left them. He saw the viewer, sitting upright, just as he had left it. And why shouldn't it be? he wondered. Why shouldn't it be?

He got up, showered and dressed, went down to the kitchen, ate breakfast and left for school.

But for once, bright as he was, Tristan could not concentrate. He felt restless, eager to be at home. Eager to look, once again into the haunting world of the viewer.

Alone in his room that afternoon, Tristan did not attempt to do his homework. He picked up the viewer, inserted the first disc again, and held the machine to his eyes.

He heard the slapping of the sea, the wind whistling through sails and rigging, the cries of the outcast, the imprisoned, the dying.

The first disc had changed.

So had the second.

As it rotated, he heard the thump of an engine and the
hiss of steam, the shudder of a machine gun, the blast
of a bomb.

The third disc had changed too.

It was the last.

But this final disc made no sound. No sound at all. From within the machine came only an eerie silence. A lifeless silence.

Afraid, Tristan tried to pull the viewer from his eyes, but he could not. He tried to look away, but he could not. Something compelled him to keep looking, to try — against his own wishes, his own common sense — to actually enter this thing, this machine. Or was it the machine itself which was luring him, drawing him in? Try as he might, he could not stop looking and, little by little, he found himself slipping away, slipping in, losing himself to a greater power, a power which he could not resist . . . was not even sure he wanted to resist . . . provided he could know . . . . could see . . . . more . . . . a little more . . . . a little more

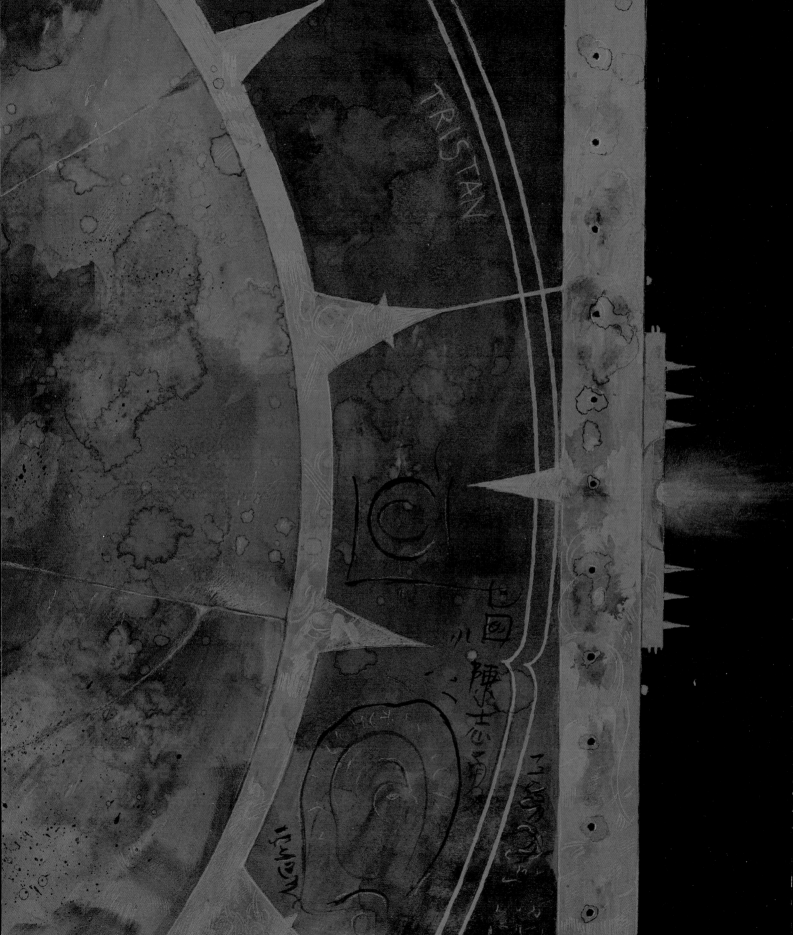

In the morning, when Tristan had not come down,
his mother called him.

There was no answer.

She went to his bedroom, knocked and went in.

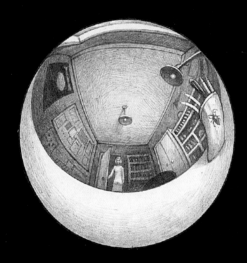

Tristan's bed was empty, but on his desk was a box,
a box of wood and metal, its lid closed,
its latch firmly locked.

which

was

curious . . .

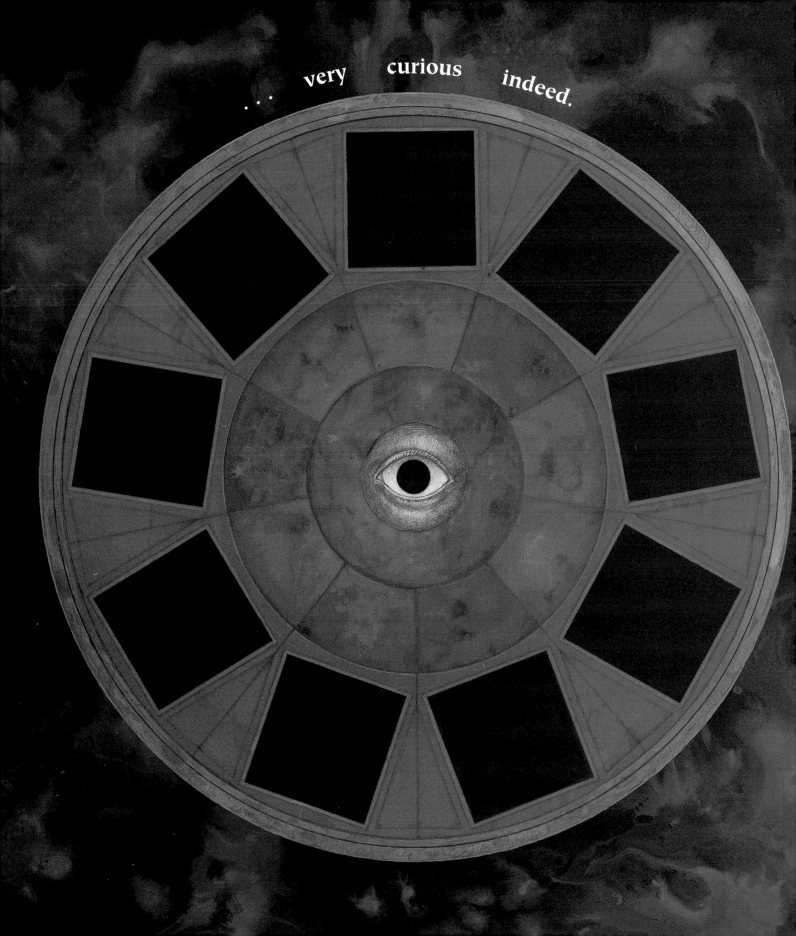

. . . very curious indeed.

DATE DUE